W9-ACN-195

WITHDRAWN

SERMONS AND SODA-WATER

III

We're Friends Again

OTHER BOOKS BY JOHN O'HARA

Appointment in Samarra

The Doctor's Son and Other Stories

Butterfield 8

Hope of Heaven

Files on Parade

Pal Joey

Pipe Night

Hellbox

A Rage to Live

The Farmers Hotel

Sweet and Sour

Ten North Frederick

A Family Party

Selected Short Stories

From the Terrace

Ourselves to Know

JOHN O'HARA

SERMONS AND SODA-WATER

III   We're Friends Again

 RANDOM HOUSE · NEW YORK

SALEM COLLEGE LIBRARY
North Carolina

First Printing
© Copyright, 1960, by John O'Hara
All rights reserved under International and Pan-American Copyright
Conventions. Published in New York by Random House, Inc., and
simultaneously in Toronto, Canada, by Random House of Canada, Limited.
Library of Congress Catalog Card Number: 60-16572
Manufactured in the United States of America

We're Friends Again

57449

I know of no quiet quite like that of a men's club at about half past nine on a summer Sunday evening. The stillness is a denial of the meaning and purpose of a club, and as you go from empty room to empty room and hear nothing but the ticking of clocks and your own heel taps on the rugless floor, you think of the membership present and past; the charming, dull, distinguished, vulgar, jolly, bibulous men who have selected this place and its company as a refuge from all other places and all other company. For that is what a club is, and to be alone in it is wrong. And at half past nine on a summer Sunday evening you are quite likely to be alone. The old men who live there have retired for the night, sure that if they die before morning they will be discovered by a chambermaid, and that if they survive this night they will have another day in which their loneliness will be broken by the lunch crowd, the cocktail crowd, and the presence of a few men in the diningroom in the evening. But on a summer Sunday evening the old men are better off in their rooms, with their personal possessions, their framed photographs and trophies of accomplishment and favorite books. The lounge, the library, the billiard and card rooms have a deathly emptiness on summer Sunday evenings, and the old men need no additional reminder of emptiness or death.

It is always dark in my club at half past nine in the evening, and darker than ever on Sunday in summer, when only the fewest possible lights are left burning. If you go to the bar the bartender slowly folds his newspaper, which he has been reading by the light from the back-bar, takes off his glasses, says "Good evening," and unconsciously looks up at the clock to see how much longer he must stay. Downstairs another club servant is sitting at the telephone switchboard. There is the spitting buzz of an incoming call and he says, " 'Devening, St. James Club? . . . No sir, he isn't . . . No sir, no message for you . . . Mr. Crankshaw went to bed about an hour ago. Orders not to disturb him, sir . . . You're welcome. Goodnight." The switchboard buzzes, the loudest, the only noise in the club, until the man pulls out the plug and the weight pulls the cord back into place, and then it is quiet again.

I had been a member of the St. James for about ten years, but I could not recall ever having been there on a Sunday until this night a year or so ago. I was summoned on the golf course by an urgent message to call the New York operator, which I did immediately. "Jim, I'm sorry to louse up your golf, but can you get a train in to New York? I don't advise driving. The traffic is terrible."

"There's a train that will get me to Penn Station about eight-thirty," I said. "But what's this all about?"

The man I was speaking to was Charles Ellis, one of my best friends.

"Charley? What's it all *about?*" I repeated.

"Nancy died this afternoon. She had a stroke after lunch."

"Oh, no. Charley, I can't tell you—"

"I know, and thanks. Are you still a member at the St. James?"

"Yes, why?"

"Will you meet me there? I'll tell you why when I see you."

"Of course. What time will you get there?"

"As soon after eight-thirty as I can."

For a little while the stillness of the club was a relief from the noise and unpleasantness of the train, which was filled with men and women and children who had presumably been enjoying themselves under the Long Island sun but were now beginning to suffer from it, and if not from the damage to their skin, from the debilitating effects of too much picnic food and canned beer. At Jamaica there was an angry scramble as we changed trains, and all the way from Jamaica to Penn Station five men fought over some fishing tackle on the car platform while three young men with thick thatches and blue jeans tormented two pansies in imitation Italian silk suits.

The bartender gave me some cold cuts and bread and cheese and made me some instant coffee. "How late do you work, Fred?" I said.

"Sundays I'm off at ten," he said, looking at the clock for the fifth or sixth time. "Don't seem worth the while, does it?"

"I'm expecting a friend, he's not a member."

"Then if I was you I'd make sure Roland knows about it. He's just as liable to fall asleep. You know, asleep at the switchboard? You heard the old saying, asleep at the switch. That fellow can go to sleep with his eyes open."

"I've already spoken to him," I said. I wandered about in the lounge and the library, not to be out of earshot when Charley Ellis arrived. As all the clocks in the club struck ten Fred came to me, dressed for the street, and said: "Can I get you anything before I go?"

"Can you let me have a bottle of Scotch?"

"I can do that, and a bowl of ice. You want soda, Mr. Malloy?"

"Just the Scotch and the ice, thanks."

"About the only place you can drink it is in your room, if you want water with it. I have to close up the bar."

"It's all right if we sit here, isn't it?"

"Jesus, if you *want* to," said Fred.

At that moment Charles Ellis arrived, escorted by Roland.

"Oh, it's Mr. Ellis," said Fred. "Remember me? Fred, from the Racquet Club?"

"Yes, hello, Fred. Is this where you are now?"

"Six and a half years," said Fred.

"Thanks very much, Fred," I said. "Goodnight."

"I'll bring you the bottle," said Fred.

"I don't want a drink, if that's what you mean," said Charles Ellis. "Unless *you've* fallen off the wagon."

"Then never mind, thanks, Fred. Goodnight."

Fred left, and I switched on some lights in the lounge.

"You saddled with that bore?" said Charley.

"I don't see much of him," I said.

"I'm sorry I'm so late. I got here as soon as I could. I called this number but it didn't answer."

"That's all right. I guess Roland had the buzzer turned off."

"Hell of an imposition, taking you away from golf and so forth. How is Kay?"

"Very distressed, naturally. She said to give you her love."

"I almost asked her to come in with you."

"She almost came," I said. "But she has her grand-children coming tomorrow."

He was silent, obviously wondering where to begin.

"Take your time," I said.

He looked up at me and smiled. "Thanks." He reached over and patted my knee. "Thanks for everything, Jim."

"Well, what the hell?"

"First, why did I want to see you here? Because I didn't want to ask you to come to the apartment, and I didn't want to go to the Racquet Club."

"I figured something like that."

"How did it happen, and all that? Nancy and I were spending the weekend at her uncle's. We went out to dinner last night, and when we came home she said she had a headache, so I gave her some aspirin. This morn-ing she still had the headache and I asked her if she wanted me to send for a doctor, but she didn't. She said she hadn't slept very well, and I probably should have called the doctor, but I didn't. Then there were four guests for lunch and I didn't have a chance to speak to her. In fact the last thing I said to her was before lunch, I told her that if she didn't feel better after lunch, she should make her excuses and lie down. And that's what she did. She excused herself, shook her head to me not to follow her, and about twenty minutes later the maid came and told us she was dead. Found her lying on the bathroom floor. I can't believe it. I can't be devoid of feeling, but I just can't believe it."

"Did the doctor give you anything?"

"You mean sedative? Tranquilizers? No, I haven't needed anything. I guess I must be in some sort of shock."

"Where are the children?"

"Well, of course Mike is in Germany, still in the Army. And I finally located Janey about an hour ago, at a house in Surrey where she's spending the weekend. She's been abroad all summer. She's flying home tomorrow and Mike has applied for leave. The Army or the Red Cross or somebody will fly him home in time for the funeral." He paused.

"Wednesday morning at eleven o'clock. Church of the Epiphany, on York Avenue. I decided Wednesday so that Mike could be here, in case there's any hitch." He looked about him. "You couldn't ask for a gloomier place than this, could you?"

"No, it's certainly appropriate."

"Well, what do I do now, Jim? You've been through it."

"Yes, I've been through it. The answer is, you're going to be so damn busy with details the next few weeks that you won't have too much time to know what hit you. You're going to find out how really nice people can be. Maybe you haven't thought about that lately, but you're going to find out. You're also going to find out that some people are shits. Real shits. I'll give you the two worst. The old friend that won't make any effort at all except maybe to send you a telegram, if that. You'll be shocked by that, so you ought to be prepared for it. I mean very close friends, guys and women you grew up with that just won't come near you. Then there's the second type, just as bad. He'll write you a letter in a week or two, and it'll be all about himself. How sad *he* is, how well he knew Nancy, how much he appreciated her, and rather strongly implying that *you* didn't know her true worth as well as he did. You'll read one of those letters and reread it, and if you do what I did, you'll throw it in the wastebasket. But the next time you see the son of a bitch, he'll say, 'Hey, Ellis, I wrote you a letter. Didn't

SALEM COLLEGE LIBRARY
Winston-Salem, North Carolina

you ever get it?' So be prepared for those two. But against them, the nice people. The *kind* people, Charley, sometimes where you'd least expect it. A guy that I thought was about as cold a fish as there is in the world, he turned out to have more real heart than almost anybody. In my book he can never do another wrong thing. The third group I haven't mentioned. The lushes. But they're obvious and you can either put up with them or brush them off. The only advice I can give you—keep busy. Don't take any more time off from your work than you absolutely have to."

"And when will it really hit me?"

"I don't know when, but I know how. Suddenly, and for no apparent reason. When your guard is down. You'll be in the subway, or walking along the street, not any favorite street full of memories, but any anonymous street. Or in a cab. And the whole God damn thing will come down on you and you'll be weeping before you know it. That's where nobody can help you, because it's unpredictable and you'll be alone. It'll only happen when you're relaxed and defenseless. But you're not relaxed, really. It's just that you're weak, *been* weakened without realizing what it's taken out of you. Emotional exhaustion, I guess it is. Then there are two other things, but I won't talk about them now. They may not happen to you, and I've told you enough."

"Thanks, Jim."

"Charley, you know what let's do? Let's go for a walk. We won't run into anybody."

"Yes. Nothing against your club, but I think I've had it here."

So the two of us went for a not too brisk walk, down Fifth Avenue, up Fifth Avenue, and to the door of Charley's apartment house. The doorman saluted him and said: "Sorry fur yur trouble, Mr. Ellis. A foine lovely woman, none foiner."

I happened, and only happened, to be looking at Charley as the doorman spoke. He nodded at the door-man but did not speak. I took his arm and led him to the elevator. "Mr. Ellis's apartment," I said, and frowned the elevator man into silence. He understood.

We got off at Charley's floor, the only apartment on that floor, and he went to the livingroom and sat down and wept without covering his face. I stayed in the foyer. Five minutes passed and then he said: "Okay,

Jim. I'm okay now. What can I give you? Ginger ale?
Coke? Glass of milk?"

"A ginger ale."

"It hit me sooner than we expected," he said. "Do you
know what it was? Or what I think it was? It was the
doorman saying nice things, and he didn't really know
her at all. He's only been here a few weeks. He doesn't
know either of us very well. Why don't you stay here
tonight, instead of going back to that God damn dreary
place?"

"I will if you'll go to bed. And don't worry, you'll
sleep."

"Will I?"

"Yes, you'll sleep tonight. Twenty blocks to a mile,
we walked damn near four miles, I make it. Take a
lukewarm tub and hit the sack. I'll read for a while and
I'll be in Mike's room. Goodnight, Charley."

"Goodnight, Jim. Thanks again."

One afternoon in 1937 I was having breakfast in my
apartment in East Fifty-fifth Street. I had worked the
night before until dawn, as was my custom, and I was
smoking my third cigarette and starting on my second

quart of coffee when the house phone rang. Charley Ellis was in the vestibule. I let him in and he shook his head at me in my pajamas, unshaven, and with the coffee and newspapers beside my chair. "La Vie de Bohème," he said.

"That's right," I said. "Come on out, Mimi, and stop that damn coughing."

Charley looked at me with genuine alarm. "You haven't got a dame here, have you? I'm sorry if—"

"No dame."

"I don't want to interrupt anything."

"I wouldn't have let you in," I said. "But I've just been reading about you, so maybe I would have. Curiosity. Who is Nancy Preswell?"

"Oh, you saw that, did you? Well, she's the wife of a guy named Jack Preswell."

"All right, who is *Jack* Preswell?" I said. "Besides being the husband of a girl named Nancy Preswell."

"Well, you've met him. With me. Do you remember a guy that we went to the ball game with a couple of years ago?"

"I do indeed. I remember everything about him but his name. A very handsome guy, a little on the short

side. Boyish-looking. And now I know who she is because I've seen them together, but I never could remember his name. Not that it mattered. He didn't
remember me at all, but she's quite a beauty. Not *quite*
a beauty. She *is* a beauty. And you're the home-wrecker."

"According to Maury Paul I am, if you believe what
he writes."

"He's often right, you know," I said. "He had me in
his column one time with a woman I'd never met, but I
met her a year or so later and he turned out to be a
very good prophet. So it's only your word against his."

"I didn't come here to be insulted," he said, taking a
chair.

"Well, what did you come here for? I haven't seen or
heard from you in God knows how long." It always took
a little while for Charley Ellis to get started on personal
matters, and if I didn't talk a lot or kid him, he would
sometimes go away without saying what he had in-
tended to say. "Now I understand *why*, of course, but
I gather Mrs. Preswell hasn't even gone to Reno yet."

"If you'll lay off this heavy-handed joshing, I guess
you'd call it, I'd like to talk seriously for a minute."

"All right. Have a cup of coffee, or do you want a
drink? If you want a drink, you know where it is."

"I don't want anything but your respectful attention and maybe some sound advice. What I really want is someone to talk to, to talk things out with."

Charley Ellis was about thirty-three years old then, and not a young thirty-three. He had stayed single because he had been in love with his first cousin, a lovely girl who was the wife of Junior Williamson, Ethridge B. Williamson, Junior; he had wanted to write, and instead had gone to work for his father's firm, Willetts & Ellis. His father knew about the second frustration, but I was now more convinced than ever that I was the only person to whom Charley had confided both.

"You may be right, you know," he said. "I probably am the home-wrecker. At least a good case could be made out against me. Nancy and Jack never have got along very well, and made no secret of the fact. But I guess I'm the first one that shall we say took advantage of the situation. They had a couple of trial separations but they always went back together until I happened to come into the picture during the last one."

"But you're not blaming yourself or anything like that, I hope."

"Not one bit. That's a form of boasting, or so it always seemed to me."

"And to me, too. That's why I'm glad you're not doing the *mea culpa* act."

"Oh, hell no. I didn't create the situation," he said.

"Do you know who did?"

"Yes, I do," said Charley. "Franklin D. Roosevelt, your great pal."

"Yeah. The inventor of bubonic plague and the common cold, and now the louser-up of the Preswell marriage. You've been spending too much time at Willetts & Ellis. You ought to come up for air."

"You were bound to say something like that, but it happens to be a fact. Preswell was one of the bright young boys that went to Washington five years ago, and that didn't sit too well with Nancy or her family. Then two years ago Preswell himself saw the light and got out, but he'd made a lot of enemies while he was defending Roosevelt, and he came back to New York hating everybody. He said to me one time, 'They call me a traitor to my class, like the Glamor Boy himself, but my class has been a traitor to me.' He used to go around telling everybody that they ought to be grateful to him, that he and Roosevelt were holding the line for the American system. But then when he quit, he was just as violent against Roosevelt as anybody, but nobody would listen. He'd been so God damn arrogant when he was *with* Roosevelt, said a lot of personal things, so nobody cared whose side he was on. And of course he began to take it out on Nancy."

"What does this gentleman do for a living?"

"He *was* with Carson, Cass & Devereux, but they don't want him back. That's just the point. Nobody wants him."

"Was he a good lawyer?"

"Well, *Harvard Law Review*, assistant editor, I think. I don't really know how good a lawyer he was. With a firm like Carson, Cass, you don't get any of the big stuff till you've been there quite a while. He has nothing to worry about financially. His father left him very well fixed and Nancy has money of her own. Her father was, or *is*, Alexander McMinnies, Delaware Zinc."

"Oh, that old crook."

"Why do you say that? You don't know whether he's a crook or a philanthropist."

"He could be both, but even if he is your girl's father, Charley, you know damn well what he is. I'll bet the boys at Carson, Cass have sat up many a night trying to keep him out of prison."

"And succeeded, in spite of Roosevelt and Homer S. Cummings."

"Those things take time," I said.

"Get your facts right. Mr. McMinnies won in the Supreme Court. Unless you were looking forward to the day when Franklin D. decides to abolish the courts and all the rest of that stuff. Which is coming, I have very little doubt."

"You don't really think that, but you have proved beyond a doubt that Roosevelt loused up Preswell's marriage. Aren't you grateful?"

"You're a tricky bastard."

"It's so easy with you guys. You have a monomania about Roosevelt."

"Monophobia."

"No, wise guy. Monophobia means fear of being alone. So much for you and your four years at the Porcellian."

"I could correct you on that four years, but I hate to spoil your good time."

"All right, we're even," I said. "What's on your mind, Charley?"

"Yes, we can't even have a casual conversation without getting into politics," he said. "Can we forget about politics?"

"Sure, I like to rib you, but what's on your mind? Nancy Preswell, obviously."

He was smoking a cigarette, and rubbing the ashes from the glowing end into the ash tray as they formed, turning the cigarette in his fingers. And not looking at *me*. "Jim, I read a short story of yours a few months ago. Nancy read it, too. She liked it, and she said she'd like to meet you. It was that story about two people at a skiing place."

"Oh, yes. 'Telemark.' "

"That's the one," he said. "They agree to get married even though they weren't in love. Was that based on your own experience—if you don't mind my asking?"

"No. I was in love when I got married, we both were. But it didn't last. No, that story was invention on my part. Well, not all invention. What is? When I was in Florida two years ago I saw this couple always together and always talking so earnestly, so seriously, and I began to wonder what they were talking about. So I thought about them, forgot them, and remembered them again and changed the locale to a skiing place, and that was the story."

"Nancy liked the story, but she didn't agree with you. You seemed to imply that they *should* have gotten married."

"Yes, I believe that, and they did."

"That's what Nancy didn't agree with. She said they were both willing to face the fact that they weren't in love, but where they were dishonest was in thinking they could make a go of it without being in love."

"I didn't imply that they'd make a go of it," I said. "But it seemed to me they had a chance. Which is as much as any two people have."

"I didn't get that, and neither did Nancy. We both thought you were practically saying that this was as good a start as two people could have."

"So far, so good, but that's *all* I implied."

"Do you think they *really* had a chance? Nancy says no. That marriage hasn't any chance without love, and not too much of a chance with it."

"Well, what do you think? How do you feel about it?"

"I wasn't ready for that question."

"I know damn well you weren't, Charley, and that's

what's eating you. It may also be what's eating Nancy. Does she know you were in love with Polly Williamson?"

"Never. You're the only one that knows that. But here I am, thirty-three, Jim. Why can't I get rid of something that never *was* anything?"

"Go to Polly and tell her that you've always been in love with her, and can't be in love with anyone else."

"I'm afraid to," he said, and smiled. "Maybe I'm afraid she'll say she feels the same way, and divorce Junior."

"Well, that's not true. She doesn't feel the same way, or you'd have found out before this. But if you admit to yourself that you're afraid, then I think you don't really love Polly as much as you think you do, or like to think you do. I was in love with Polly for one afternoon, and I told her so. I meant it, every word of it. But every now and then I see her with Williamson and I thank God she had some sense. A girl with less sense might conceivably have divorced Williamson and married me, and how long would that have lasted? Polly is Williamson's wife, prick though he may be. And if she wants Williamson, she certainly doesn't want me, and probably not you. Has Polly ever stepped out on her own?"

"I think she did, with a guy from Boston. An older guy. I don't think you'd even know his name. A widower, about forty-five. Not a playboy type at all. Very serious-minded. Just right for Polly. You know, Polly has her limitations when it comes to a sense of humor, the lighter side. She was born here, but her father and mother both came from Boston and she's always been more of a Boston type than New York. Flowers and music and the children. But she does her own work in the garden, and she often goes to concerts by herself. What I'm saying is, no *chi-chi*. She's a good athlete, but there again it isn't what you might call public sport. The contest is always between her and the game itself, and the things she's best at are games like golf or trap-shooting. Skiing. Figure-skating. Polly damn near doesn't need anyone else to enjoy herself. And God knows she never needed me." He paused. "Did you ever hear her play the piano?"

"No."

"She's good. You know, Chopin. Rachmaninoff. Tschaikovsky."

"Charley, I just discovered something about you," I said.

"What?"

"*You're* a Bostonian."

"Maybe."

"The admiring way you talk about Polly, and of course you're a first cousin. Isn't it practically a tradition in Boston that you fall in love with your first cousin?"

"It's been known to happen, but I assure you, it had nothing to do with my falling in love with Polly."

"Do you mind if I take issue with you on that point? I have a theory that it had a *lot* to do with your falling in love with Polly, and that your present love affair, with Nancy, is your New York side."

He laughed. "Oh, God. How facile, and how stupid . . . I take back stupid, but you're wrong."

"Why am I wrong? You haven't given the theory any thought. And I have, while listening to you. You'd better give it some thought, and decide whether you want to be a New Yorker or a Bostonian."

"Or you might be wrong and I won't have to make the choice."

"Yes, but don't reject my theory out of hand. You're a loner. You wanted to be a writer. You're conventional, as witness working in the family firm against your will,

but doing very well I understand. And you were talking about yourself as much as you were about Polly."

"Not at all. I was a great team-sport guy. Football in
school, and rowing in college."

"Rowing. The obvious joke. Did you ever meet that
Saltonstall fellow that rowed Number 5?"

"I know the joke, and it was never very funny to us. A
Yale joke. Or more likely Princeton." He seemed to ig-
nore me for a moment. He sat staring at his outstretched
foot, his elbow on the arm of his chair, his cheek resting
on the two first fingers of his left hand while the other
two fingers were curled under the palm. "And yet, you
may have a point," he said, judicially. "You just may
have a point. Dr. Jekyll and Mr. Hyde. Larry Lowell and
Jimmy Walker. Waldo Emerson and Walter Winchell.
This conversation may be the turning point of my whole
life, and I'll owe it all to you, you analytical son of a
bitch."

"That's the thanks I get. Watery compliments."

He rose. "Gotta go," he said.

"How come you're uptown at this hour?"

"I took the afternoon off," he said. "I have a perfectly
legitimate reason for being uptown, but I know your

nasty mind. Will you be in town next week? How about dinner Tuesday?"

"Tuesday, no. Wednesday, yes."

"All right, Wednesday. Shall we pick you up here? I'd like Nancy to see the squalor you live in."

"Others have found it to have a certain Old World charm," I said. "All right, Mimi. You can come out now."

"Listen, don't have any Mimi here Wednesday, will you, please?"

"That's why I said Wednesday instead of Tuesday."

"Degrading. And not even very instructive," he said.

"Not if you don't want to learn."

My apartment was actually a comfortable, fairly expensively furnished two rooms and bath, which was cleaned daily by a colored woman who worked full-time elsewhere in the building. But Charley Ellis's first remark when he arrived with Nancy Preswell was: "Why, look, he's had the place all spruced up. Is all this new?"

"All goes back to Sloane's in the morning," I said. "How do you do, Mrs. Preswell?"

"Wait a minute. You haven't been introduced," said Charley. "You could have put me in a hell of a spot. What if this hadn't been Mrs. Preswell?" He was in high good humor, determined to make this a pleasant evening.

"I often wish I weren't," she said, without bitterness, but as her first words to me they were an indication that she knew Charley confided in me. "By the way, how do you do?"

"I've often seen you. Well, pretty often," I said.

"And always pretty," said Charley.

I looked at him and then at her: "You've done wonders with this guy. I hardly recognize the old clod." My remark pleased her, and she smiled affectionately at Charley. "Gallantry, yet," I said.

"It was always there," said Charley. "It just took the right person to bring it out."

"I like your apartment, Mr. Malloy. Is this where you do all your writing?"

"Most of it. Practically all of it."

"Oh, you type your stories?" she said, looking at my typewriter. "But don't you write them in longhand first?"

"No. I don't even write letters in longhand."

"Love letters?"

"I type them," I said.

"And mimeographs them," said Charley. "Shall we have a free drink here, saving me two and a quarter?"

"The market closed firm, but have you ever noticed that Charley hates to part with a buck?"

"No, that's not fair," said Nancy Preswell.

"Or true. What's the name of that friend of yours, that writes the Broadway stories?"

"Mark Hellinger?"

"Hellinger. Right. I thought he was going to have a stroke that night when I paid a check at '21.'"

"I very nearly had one myself."

"No, now that isn't fair," said Nancy Preswell.

"I'm softening him up for later," I said.

We had some drinks and conversation, during which Nancy slowly walked around, looking at my bookshelves and pictures. "I gather you don't like anything very modern," she said.

"Not in this room. Some abstract paintings in the bathroom."

"May I see your bedroom?"

"Believe me, that's the best offer he's had today," said Charley.

"A four-poster," she said.

"Early Wanamaker," I said. "*Circa* 1930."

"All you need is a rag rug and a cat curled up on it. I like it. That's not your father, is it?"

"My grandfather. Practically everything in this room is a copy of stuff I remember from when I was a kid. I depended entirely on their taste."

"But you bought it all yourself, so it's your taste, too," said Nancy Preswell. "Very interesting, and very revealing, considering what some of the critics say about your writings."

"What does it reveal to you?" I said.

"That basically you're very conventional."

"I could have told you that," I said.

"Yes, but I probably wouldn't have believed you if I hadn't seen your apartment."

"I think I ought to tell you, though. I went through an all-modernistic phase when I lived in the Village."

"Why are you for Roosevelt?" she said.

"No! Not tonight, please," said Charley.

"You shouldn't be, you know," she persisted.

"Shall we not argue about it? I'm for him, and you're not, and that's where we'd be if we argued till to-morrow morning," I said.

"Except that I think I could convince you. You don't know my husband, do you? I know you've met him, but you've never talked with him about Roosevelt."

"When was *he* most convincing?" I said. "When he was with him, or against him?"

"He was never in the least convincing when he was for him. And he's not very convincing now. But as a writer you should be able to disregard a lot of things he says and go beneath the surface. Then you'd see what a man like Roosevelt can do to an idealist. And my husband *was* an idealist."

"Don't look at me. I'm not saying a word," said Charley.

"I do look at you, for corroboration. Jack *was* an idealist. You may not have liked him, but you have to admit that."

"Yes, he was," said Charley.

"And so were you. But Jack did something about it. You played it safe."

"Jim is wondering why I'm not taking this big. The reason is we've had it out before," said Charley.

"Many times," said Nancy Preswell. "And probably will again."

"But not tonight, shall we?" said Charley Ellis.

"I hate Mr. Roosevelt," she said. "And I can't stand it when a writer that I think is good is *for* him. I'm one of those people that think he ought to be assassinated, and I just hope somebody else does it, not my poor, drunken, disillusioned husband."

"Is he liable to, your husband?" I said.

"I don't suppose there's any real danger of it. But it's what he thinks of day and night. I don't want you to think I love my husband. I haven't for years. But Jack Preswell was an idealist, and Roosevelt turned him into a fanatic."

"He might have been a fanatical idealist."

"*He was!* Four years ago, that's what he was. But there's nothing left now but the fanaticism. Don't you see that, Mr. Malloy? Mr. Roosevelt took away his ideals."

"How are you on ideals, Mrs. Preswell?"

"If that's supposed to be a crusher, it isn't . . . I have a few, but they're not in any danger from—that awful man. Now I've said enough, and you probably don't want to have dinner with us."

"Yes, I would. You're a very attractive girl."

"As long as I don't say what I think? That's insulting, and now I'm not sure *I* want to have dinner with *you*."

There was a silence, broken by Charley: "Well, what shall we do? Toss a coin? Heads we dine together, tails we separate."

"I'll agree to an armistice if Mr. Malloy will."

"All right," I said. "Let's go. Maybe if we have a change of scenery . . ."

"I promise I'll be just as stupid as you want me to be," said Nancy Preswell.

There was not another word about politics all evening, and at eleven o'clock we took a taxi to a theatre where I was to meet an actress friend of mine, Julianna Moore, the female heavy in an English mystery play. Julie was about thirty, a girl who had been prematurely starred after one early success, and had never again found the right play. Her father was a history professor at Yale, and Julie was a well-educated girl whom I had first known in our Greenwich Village days. We had been lovers then, briefly, but now she was a friend of my ex-wife's and the mistress of a scenic designer.

Nancy Preswell began with compliments to Julie, ticking off six plays in which Julie had appeared.

"You must go to the theatre all the time, to have seen some of those sad little turkeys," said Julie.

"I go a lot," said Nancy.

"Did you ever do any acting?"

"*Did* I? 'Shall I speak ill of him that is my husband?/ Ah, poor my lord, what tongue shall smooth thy name . . .'"

"'When I, thy three-hours wife, have mangled it?' Where and when did you do Juliet?" said Julie.

"At Foxcroft."

"I'll bet you were a very pretty Juliet," said Julie.

"Thank you. If I was, that says it all. I was cured."

"Well, I was the kind of ham that never was cured, if you don't mind a very small joke . . . I always thought it would have been fun to go to Foxcroft. All that riding and drilling."

"Where *did* you go?"

"A Sacred Heart school in Noroton, Connecticut, then two years at Vassar."

"Where did you go to school, Charley," I said.

"I don't know. Where did you?" he said.

"Oh, a Sacred Heart school in Noroton, Connecticut. Then two years at Foxcroft," I said.

"Too tarribly fonny, jost too tarribly fonny," said Julie.

"That's her Mickey Rooney imitation. Now do Lionel Barrymore," I said.

"Too tarribly fonny, jost too tarribly fonny," said Julie.

"Isn't she good?" I said. "Now do Katharine Hepburn."

"Who?" said Julie.

"She's run out of imitations," I said.

We went to "21," the 18 Club, LaRue, and El Morocco. We all had had a lot to drink, and Julie, who had played two performances that day, had soon caught up with the rest of us by drinking double Scotches. "Now the big question is, the all-important question—*is*," said Julie.

"What is the big question, Julie dear?" said Nancy.

"Ah, you like me, don't you? I like you, too," said Julie. "I like Charley, too. And I used to like Jim, didn't I, Jim?"

"Used to, but not any more."

"Correct. Jim is a rat. Aren't you, Jim?"

"Of course he's a rat," said Nancy. "He's a Franklin D. Roosevelt rat."

"I'm a Franklin D. Roosevelt rat. You be careful what you say," said Julie.

"The hell with that. What was the big question?" said Charley.

"*My* big question?" said Julie.

"Yes," said Charley.

"I didn't know I had one. Oh, yes. The big *question. Is.* Do we go to Harlem and I can't go on tomorrow night and I give my understudy a break. *Or. Or.* Do I go home to my trundle bed—and you stay out of it, Jim. You're a rat. I mean stay out of my trundle. Nevermore, quoth the raven. Well, what did my understudy ever do for me? So I guess we better go home. Right?"

"Yeah. I haven't got an understudy," said Charley. He signaled for the check.

"Jim, why are you such a rat? If you weren't such a rat. But that's what you are, a rat," said Julie.

"Pretend I'm not a rat."

"How can I pretend a thing like that? I'm the most promising thirty-year-old ingénue there is, but I can't pretend you're not a rat. Because that's what you are. Your ex-wife is my best friend, so what else are you but' a rat? Isn't that logical, Jim? Do you remember Bank Street? That was before you were a rat."

"No, I was a rat then, Julie."

"No. No, you weren't. If you were a rat then, you wouldn't be one now. That's logical."

"But he's not a bad rat," said Nancy.

"Oh, there you're wrong. If he was a good little rat I'd take him home with me. But I don't want a rat in my house."

"Then you come to my house," I said.

"All right," said Julie. "That solves everything. I don't know *why* I didn't think of that before. Remember Bank Street, Jim?"

"Sure."

She stood up. "*Good*night, Nancy. *Good*night, Charley." On her feet she became dignified, the star. She held her mink so that it showed her to best advantage and to the captains who said, "Goodnight, Miss Moore," she nodded and smiled. In the taxi she was ready to be kissed. "Ah, Jim, what a Christ-awful life, isn't it? You won't tell Ken, will you?"

"No. I won't tell anybody."

"Just don't tell Ken. I don't want him to think I care

that much. He's giving me a bad time. Kiss me, Jim. Tell me I'm nicer than Nancy."

"You're much nicer than Nancy. Or anybody else."

She smiled. "You're a rat, Jim, but you're a nice old rat. It's all right if I call you a rat, isn't it? Who the hell is she to say you aren't a bad rat? She's not in our game, is she?"

"No."

"We don't have to let her in our game. But *he* does, the poor son of a bitch."

When she saw my bedroom she said: "Good Lord, Jim, I feel pregnant already. That's where Grandpa and Grandma begat. Isn't it? I hope *we* don't beget."

I was still asleep when she left, and on my desk there was a note from her:

Dear Rat:

You didn't use to snore on Bank Street. Am going home to finish my sleep. It is eight-fifteen and you seem good for many more hours. I had a lovely time and have the hangover to prove it. Want to be home in case K. calls as he said he would. In any case we are better off than Nancy and Charles. Are they headed for trouble! ! !

Love,

J.

P. S.: The well-appointed bachelor's apartment has a supply of extra toothbrushes. My mouth tastes like the inside of the motorman's glove. Ugh! ! !

J.

The motorman's glove. Passé collegiate slang of the previous decade, when the word whereupon was stuck into every sentence and uzza-mattera-fact and wet-smack and swell caught on and held on. I read Julie's note a couple of times, and "the motorman's glove" brought to mind two lines from *Don Juan* that had seemed strangely out of character for Byron:

> Let us have wine and women, mirth and laughter,
> Sermons and soda-water the day after.

The mirth and laughter, the wine and women were not out of character, but there was something very vulgar about Byron's taking soda-water for a hangover as I took Eno's fruit salts. An aristocrat, more than a century dead, and a man I disliked as cordially as if he were still alive. But he had said it all, more than a hundred years ago. I made a note to buy a copy of *Don Juan* and send it, with that passage marked, to Julie. At that moment, though, I was trying to figure out what she meant by Nancy and Charley, headed for trouble. There was trouble already, and more to come.

I waited until four o'clock and then telephoned Julie. "It's the rat," I said. "How are you feeling?"

"I'll live. I'll be able to go on tonight. Actually, I'm feeling much better than I have any right to, considering the amount I drank. I went home and took a bath and fiddled around till Ken called—"

"He called, did he?"

"Yes. There isn't going to be anything in the columns about you and me, is there?"

"My guess is a qualified no. If we went out again tonight there would be, but—"

"But we're not going out again tonight," she said. "I don't have to tell you that last night was a lapse."

"You don't have to, but you did," I said.

"Now don't get huffy," she said. "It wouldn't have happened with anyone else, and it wouldn't have happened with you if it hadn't been for the old days on Bank Street."

"I know that, Julie, and I'm not even calling you for another date. I want to know what you meant by—I have your note here—Nancy and Charley headed for trouble. Was something said? Did something happen that I missed?"

"Oh, God, I have to think. It seems to me I wrote that ages ago. And it was only this morning. Is it important? I could call you back?"

"Not important."

"*I* know. I know what it was. Is Nancy's husband a man named Jack Preswell?"

"Yes."

"Well, he was at Morocco last night. Standing at the bar all alone and just staring at us. Staring, staring, staring. I used to know him when I was a prom-trotter, back in the paleolithic age."

"How did you happen to see him and we didn't?"

"Because I was facing that way and you weren't," she said. "Maybe I should have said something. Maybe I did."

"No, you didn't."

"I don't think I did. No, I guess I didn't, because now I remember thinking that I wasn't positively sure it was he. But when you and I left I caught a glimpse of him, and it was. If anybody was tighter than we were, he was. His eyes were just barely open, and he was holding himself up by the elbows. I'll bet he didn't last another ten minutes."

"Well, just about," I said.

"What do you mean?"

"Have you seen the early editions of the afternoon papers?"

"No. I don't get the afternoon papers here."

"Preswell was hit by a taxi at 54th and Lexington. Fractured his skull and died before the ambulance got there. According to the cops he just missed being hit by a northbound cab, and then walked in front of a southbound. Four or five witnesses said the hack driver was not at fault, which is another way of saying Preswell was blind drunk."

"Well, I guess I could almost swear to that, but I'm glad I don't have to. I won't, will I?"

"Not a chance. He wasn't with us, and none of us ever spoke to him. The *Times* and the *Trib* will print the bare facts and people can draw their own conclusions. The *News* and the *Mirror* will play it up tonight, but it's only a one-day story. However, there is one tabloid angle. If the *Mirror* or the *News* finds out that Nancy was in Morocco with Charley—well, they could do something with that."

"And would you and I get in the papers?"

"Well, if I were the city editor of the *News* or the *Mirror,* and a prominent actress and an obscure author—"

"Oh, Lord. And I told Ken I went straight home from the theatre. Jim, you know a lot of those press people . . ."

"Julie, if they find out, your picture's going to be in the tabloids. I couldn't prevent that."

"And they *are* going to find out, aren't they?"

"The only straight answer is yes. You spoke to a lot of people as we were leaving. Waiter captains. People at the tables. If you can think of a story to tell Ken, I'll back you up. But maybe the best thing is to tell him the truth, up to a certain point."

"He'll supply the rest, after that certain point. He knows about Bank Street."

"That was eight years ago. Can't you have an evening out with an old friend?"

"Would you believe that line?"

"No," I said. "But I have a very suspicious nature."

"You're a blind man trusting a boy scout compared to Ken. He didn't believe me when I told him I went straight home from the theatre. But in the absence of proof—now he's got his proof."

"Well, then have a date with me tonight. Make the son of a bitch good and jealous."

"I'm almost tempted. When will we know about the *News* and the *Mirror?*"

"Oh, around nine o'clock tonight."

"You'll see them when they come out, before I can. If they mention me, will you stop for me at the theatre? That isn't much of an offer, Jim, but for old time's sake?"

"And if you're not mentioned, you have a date with Ken?"

"Yes," she said.

"All right. You understand, of course, this is something I wouldn't do for just anybody, take second best."

"I understand exactly why you're doing it, and so do you," she said.

"I detect the sound of *double entendre.*"

"Well, that's how I meant it. You're being nice, but you also know that nice little rats get a piece of candy.

And don't make the obvious remark about piece of what. Seriously, Jim, I can count on you, can't I?"

"I would say that you are one of the few that can always count on me, Julie. For whatever that's worth."

"Right now, a great deal."

"Well, I wish you luck, even though I'll be the loser in the deal."

"You didn't lose anything last night. And I may have lost a husband. He was talking that way today."

"Do you want to marry him?"

"Yes, I do. Very much. Too much. So much that all he ever sees is my phony indifference. Too smart for my own good, I am. Jim, ought I to call Nancy Preswell, or write her a note?"

"A note would be better, I think."

"Yes, I do, too."

"I've been calling Charley all afternoon, and nobody knows where he is. But he'll be around when he wants to see me."

"It's a hateful thing for me to say, but in a way he's stuck, isn't he?"

"He wants to be."

"He's still stuck," said Julie.

At about eleven-twenty I was standing with the backstage doorman, who was saying goodnight to the actors and actresses as they left the theatre. "Miss Moore's always one of the last to leave," he said. "We us'ally break about five to eleven, but tonight she's later than us'al. I told her you was here. I told her myself."

"That's all right," I said.

"She dresses with Miss Van, one flight up. I'll just go tell her you're here."

"No. No thanks. Don't hurry her," I said.

"She's us'ally one of the last out, but I don't know what's keeping her tonight."

"Making herself look pretty," I said.

"She's a good little actress. You know, they had to change the curtain calls so she could take a bow by herself."

There were footsteps on the winding iron stairway, the cautious, high-heeled footsteps of all actresses descending all backstage stairways, but these were made by Julie. She did not make any sign of recognition of me but took my arm. "Goodnight, Mike," she said.

"Goodnight, Miss Moore. See you tomorrow. Have a good time," said the doorman.

"Let's go where we won't see anybody. Have you got the papers? I don't mind being seen with you, Jim, but I don't want to be seen crying. As soon as Mike said 'Mr. Malloy,' I knew. Tomorrow the press agent will thank me for the publicity break. Irony."

I took her to a small bar in the New Yorker Hotel, and she read the *News* and the *Mirror*. The *Mirror* had quite a vicious little story by a man named Walter Herbert, describing the gay foursome and the solitary man at the bar of El Morocco, and leaving the unmistakable inference that Jack Preswell had stumbled out into the night and thrown himself in front of a taxi. The *News*, in a story that had two by-lines, flatly said that Preswell had gone to the night club in an attempt to effect a reconciliation with his wife, who was constantly in the company of Charles Ellis, multi-millionaire stockbroker and former Harvard oarsman, and onetime close friend of the dead man. The *Mirror* ran a one-column cut of Julie, an old photograph from the White Studios; the *News* had a more recent picture of her in the décolleté costume she wore in the play. There was a wedding picture of Preswell and Nancy in the *News,* which also came up with a manly picture of Charley Ellis in shorts, shirt, and socks, holding an oar. There was no picture of me, and in both papers the textual mention of Julie and me was almost identical: Julie was the beautiful young actress, I was the sensational young novelist.

"Were we as gay as they say we were? I guess we were," said Julie.

"The implication is, that's what happens to society people when they mix with people like you and me."

"Exactly. They only got what they deserved. By the way, what did they get, besides a little notoriety? I'm beginning to feel sorry for Preswell. I lose a possible husband, but it must hurt to be hit by a taxi, even if you do die right away."

"You're taking it very well," I said.

"I thought Ken might show up, if only to demand an explanation. He loves to demand explanations. Have you talked to Ellis?"

"No. I'd like to know if there's anything in that *News* story, about Preswell and the reconciliation. I doubt it, and nobody will sue, but either the *News* has a very good rewrite man or they may have something. If it's something dreamed up by the rewrite man he ought to get a bonus, because he's taken a not very good story and dramatized the whole scene at Morocco."

"Thank goodness for one thing. They left my father and mother out of it," she said. "Poor Daddy. He groans. He comes to see me in all my plays, and then takes me to one side and asks if it's absolutely necessary to wear such low-cut dresses, or do I always *have* to be unfaithful to my husband? He told Thornton Wilder I'd have been just right for the girl in *Our Town*. Can you imagine how I'd have had to hunch over to play a fourteen-year-old?"

We were silent for a moment and then suddenly she said: "Oh, the hell with it. Let's go to '21'?"

"I'll take you to '21,' but no night clubs."

"I want to go to El Morocco and the Stork Club."

"No, you can't do it."

"I'm not in mourning."

"I used to be a press agent, Julie. If you want to thumb your nose at Ken, okay. But if you go to El Morocco tonight, you're asking for the worst kind of publicity. Capitalizing on those stories in the *News* and *Mirror*. You're better than that."

"Oh, the hell I am."

"Well, you used to be."

"The hell with what I used to be. I was a star, too, but now I'm just a sexy walk-on. And a quick lay, for somebody that calls me up after eight years. Why *did* you take me out last night?"

"Because you're a lady, and so is Nancy."

"Oh, it was Nancy you were trying to impress? I wish I'd known *that*."

"I have no desire to impress Nancy. I merely thought you'd get along with her and she with you."

"Why? Because she did Juliet at Foxcroft?"

"Oh, balls, Julie."

"Would you say that to Nancy?"

"If she annoyed me as much as you do, yes, I would. If you'll shut up for a minute, I'll tell you something. I don't like Nancy. I think she's a bitch. But I like Charley."

"Why do you like Charley? He's not your type. As soon as you make a little money you want to join the Racquet Club and all the rest of that crap. That apartment, for God's sake! And those guns. You're not Ernest Hemingway. Would you know how to fire a gun?"

"If I had one right now I'd show you."

"When did you get to be such pals with Charley Ellis?"

"I was hoping you'd get around to that. I knew him before I knew you, before I ever wrote anything. As to the armament, the shotguns belonged to my old man, including one that he gave me when I was fourteen. I do admit I bought the rifle four years ago. As to the apartment—well, you liked it last night. If you want to feel guilty about it, go ahead. But you said yourself it was a damned sight more comfortable than that studio couch on Bank Street. What do you want to do? Do you want to go to '21' and have something to eat, or shall I take you home?" I looked at my watch.

"It isn't too late to get another girl, is it?"

"That's exactly what I was thinking."

"Some girl from one of the night clubs?"

"Yes."

"I thought they only went out with musicians and gangsters."

"That's what you thought, and you go on thinking it. Do you want to go to '21'?"

"How late can you get one of those girls?"

"Two-thirty, if I'm lucky."

"You mean if you call up now and make the date?"

"Yes."

"You're a big liar, Jim. They have a two o'clock show that lasts an hour, so you can call this girl any time between now and two o'clock, and you won't meet her till after three. I know the whole routine. A boy in our play is married to one of them."

"The girl I had in mind isn't a show girl and she isn't in the line. She does a specialty."

She put her chin in her hand and her elbow on the table, in mock close attention. "*Tell* me about her specialty, Jim. Is it something I should learn? Or does one have to be double-jointed?"

"You want to go to '21'?"

"I'm dying to go to '21'," she said.

"Well, why didn't you say so?"

"Because you're such a grump, and I had to get a lot of things out of my system."

We used each other for a couple of weeks in a synthetic romance that served well in place of the real thing; and we were conscientious about maintaining the rules and customs of the genuine. We saw only each other and formed habits: the same taxi driver from the theatre, the same tables in restaurants, exchanges of small presents and courtesies; and we spoke of the wonder of our second chance at love. It was easy to love Julie. After the first few days and nights she seemed to have put aside her disappointment as easily as I was overcoming my chronic loneliness. We slept at my apartment nearly every night, and when she stayed at hers we would talk on the telephone until there was nothing more to say. We worried about each other: I, when the closing notice was put up at her theatre, and she when a story of mine was rejected. A couple of weeks became a couple of months and our romance was duly noted in the gossip columns: we were sizzling, we were hunting a preacher. "Would you ever go back to the Church?" she said, when it was printed that we were going to marry.

"I doubt it. Would you?"

"If Daddy wanted me to get married in the Church, I would."

"We've never talked about this."

"You mean about marriage?"

"*Or* the Church. Do you want to talk about marriage?"

"Yes, I have a few things I want to say. I love you,

Jim, and you love me. But we ought to wait a long time before we do anything about getting married. If I'm married in the Church I'm going to stick to it."

"You wouldn't have with Ken."

"No, but he never was a Catholic. If I married you, in the Church, I'd want a nuptial Mass and you'd have to go to confession and the works. With a Protestant—Ken—I couldn't have had a nuptial Mass and I'd have been half-hearted about the whole thing. But marrying you would be like going back to the Church automatically. I consider you a Catholic."

"Do you consider yourself a Catholic?"

"Yes. I never go to Mass, and I haven't made my Easter duty since I was nineteen, but it's got me. I'm a Catholic."

"It's gone from me, Julie. The priests have ruined it for me."

"They've almost ruined it for me, but not quite. I don't listen to the priests. I can't tell that in confession, but that's why I stay away. Well, one of the reasons. I don't believe that going to bed with you is a sin."

"The priests do."

"Let them. They'll never be told unless I marry a

Catholic and go to confession. That's why I say we ought to wait a long time. I'm thinking of myself. If I marry a Catholic, I'll be a Catholic. If I don't I'll be whatever I am. A non-practicing member of the faithful. I'll never be anything else."

"Well, neither will I. But I'm a heretic on too many counts, and the priests aren't going to accept me on my terms. It wouldn't be the Church if they did. It would be a new organization called the Malloyists."

"I'll be a Malloyist until we get married."

"There's one thing, Julie. If you get pregnant, what?"

"If I get pregnant, I'll ask you to marry me. I've had two abortions, but the father wasn't a Catholic. It was Ken. I paid for the abortions myself and never told him I was pregnant. I didn't want to have a baby. I wanted to be a star. But if I ever get pregnant by you, I'll tell you, and I hope you'll marry me."

"I will."

"However, I've been very, very careful except for that first night."

I have never been sure what that conversation did to us. I have often thought that we were all right so long as we felt a future together without getting down to

plans, without putting conditional restrictions on ourselves, without specifying matters of time or event. It
is also quite possible that the affection and passion that
we identified as love was affection and passion and
tenderness, but whatever sweetness we could add to
the relationship, we could not add love, which is never
superimposed. In any event, Julie stayed away one
night and did not answer her telephone, and the next
day I was having my coffee and she let herself in.

"Hello," I said.

"I'm sorry, Jim."

"I suppose you came to get your things," I said. I took
a sip of coffee and lit a cigarette.

"Not only to get my things."

"You know, the awful thing is, you look so God damn
—oh, nuts." She was wearing a blue linen dress that was
as plain as a Chinese sheath, but there was more under-
neath that dress than Chinese girls have, and I was
never to have it again. Someone else had been having it
only hours ago.

"All right," I said. "Get your things."

"Aren't you going to let me say thank-you for what
we had?"

"Yes, and I thank you, Julie. But I can't be nice about last night and all this morning." I took another sip of coffee and another drag on my cigarette, and she put her hand to her face and walked swiftly out of the room. I waited a while, then got up and went to the bedroom. She was lying face down on my unmade bed and she was crying.

"You'll wrinkle your dress," I said.

"The hell with my dress," she said, and slowly turned and sat up. "Jim." She held out her arms.

"Oh, no," I said.

"I couldn't help it. He came to the theatre."

"Oh, hell, I don't want to hear about that."

"I promised him I wouldn't see you again, but I had to come here."

"No you didn't, Julie. I could have sent you your things. It would have been much better if you'd just sent me a telegram."

"Put your arms around me."

"Oh, now that isn't like you. What the hell do you think I am? I've had about two hours' sleep. I'm on the ragged edge, but you don't have to do that to me."

She stood up and slipped her dress over her head, and

took off her underclothes. "Can I make up for last night?" she said. "I'll never see you again. Will you put your arms around me now?"

"I wish I could say no, but I wanted you the minute I saw you."

"I know. That's why you wouldn't look at me, isn't it?"

"Yes."

She was smiling, and she could well afford to, with the pride she had in her breasts. "How do you want to re- member me? I'll be whatever you want."

"What is this, a performance?"

"Of course. A farewell performance. Command, too. You don't want me as a virgin, do you?"

"No."

"No, that would take too much imagination on *your* part. But I could be one if that's what you want. But you don't. You'd much rather remember me as a slut, wouldn't you?"

"Not a slut, Julie. But not a virgin. Virgin's aren't very expert."

"You'd rather remember me as an expert. A whore.

Then you'll be able to forget me and you won't have to forgive me. All right."

She knew things I had never told her and there was no love in the love-making, but when she was dressed again and had her bag packed she stood in the bed-room doorway. "Jim?"

"What?"

"I'm not like that," she said. "Don't remember me that way, please?"

"I hope I don't remember you at all."

"I love him. I'm going to marry him."

"You do that, Julie."

"Haven't you got one nice thing to say before I go?"

I thought of some cruel things and I must have smiled at the thought of them, because she began to smile too. But I shook my head and she shrugged her shoulders and turned and left. The hall door closed and I looked at it, and then I saw that the key was being pushed under it. Twenty-three crowded years later I still remember the angle of that key as it lay on the dark-green carpet. My passion was spent, but I was not calm of mind; by accident the key was pointed toward me, and I thought of the swords at a court-

martial. I was being resentenced to the old frenetic loneliness that none of us would admit to, but that governed
our habits and our lives.

In that state of mind I made a block rejection of a
thousand men and women whom I did not want to see,
and reduced my friendships to the five or ten, the three
or five, and finally the only person I felt like talking to.
And that was how I got back in the lives of Charley
Ellis and Nancy McMinnies Preswell Ellis.

They had been married about a month, and I was not
sure they would be back from their wedding trip, but
I got Charley at his office and he said he had started
work again that week. He would stop in and have a drink
on his way home.

"Gosh, the last time I was in this apartment—" he
said, and it was not necessary to go on.

"You ended up getting married, and I damn near did
myself."

"To Julia Murphy?"

"Close. Julianna Moore. In fact, your coming here
rounds out a circle, for me. She ditched me today."

"Are you low on account of it?"

"Yes, so tell me about you and Nancy. I saw the announcement of your wedding, in the papers."

"That's all there was. We didn't send out any others."

"You lose a lot of loot that way," I said.

"I know, but there were other considerations. We wanted people to forget us in a hurry, so Nancy's mother sent short announcements to the *Tribune* and the *Sun*. You can imagine we'd had our fill of the newspapers when Preswell was killed."

"I don't have to imagine. It was the start of my romance, the one that just ended." I told him what had happened, a recital which I managed to keep down to about fifteen minutes. I lied a little at the end: "So this morning she called me up and said she'd gone back to her friend Mr. Kenneth Kenworthy."

"Well, you might say our last meeting here did end in two marriages," said Charley.

"If he marries her. He's been married three times and if she marries him she's going to have to support herself. He has big alimony to pay. I hope they do get married. Selfishly. I don't want any more synthetic romances. They're just as wearing as the real thing, and as Sam Hoffenstein says, what do you get yet?"

"Everything, if it turns out all right. You remember Nancy and her theory that nobody should get married without love, the real thing? That story of yours we talked about—'Telemark'?"

"Yes."

"Well, to be blunt about it, I really forced Nancy to marry me. All that notoriety—I put it to her that if she didn't marry me, *I'd* look like a shitheel. So on that basis—"

"Oh, come on."

"It's true. That's why she took the chance. But what was true then isn't true now. I want you to be the twenty-fifth to know. We're having a child."

"She never had any by Preswell?"

"No, and she wanted one, but his chemistry was all wrong. We expect ours in March or April."

"Congratulations."

"Thank you. Needless to say, I'm an altogether different person."

"You mean you have morning sickness?"

"I mean just the opposite. I'm practically on the wagon, for one thing, and for the first time in my life

I'm thinking about someone besides myself. Get married, Malloy, and have a baby right away."

"I *like* to think about myself," I said.

"That's bullshit, and it's a pose. All this crazy life you lead, I think you're about the lonesomest son of a bitch I know."

I bowed my head and wept. "You shouldn't have said that," I said. "I wish you'd go."

"I'm sorry, Jim. I'll go. But why don't you drop in after dinner if you feel like it?"

"Thanks," I said, and he left.

He had taken me completely unawares. His new happiness and my new misery and all that the day had taken out of me made me susceptible of even the slightest touch of pity or kindness. I stopped bawling after two minutes, and then I began again, but during the second attack I succumbed to brain fag and fell asleep. I slept about three hours and was awakened by the telephone.

"This is Nancy Ellis. I hope you're coming up, we're expecting you. I'll bet you haven't had your dinner. Tell me the truth?"

"As a matter of fact, I was asleep."

"Well, how about some lamb chops? Do you like them

black on the outside and pink on the inside? And have you any pet aversions in the vegetable line?"

"Brussels sprouts. But do you mean to say you haven't had your dinner?"

"We've had ours, but I can cook. Half an hour?"

It was a pleasant suburban evening in a triplex apartment in East Seventy-first Street, with one of the most beautiful women in New York cooking my supper and serving it; and it was apparent from their avoidance of all intimate topics that they had decided how they would treat me. At ten-thirty Nancy went to bed, at eleven Charley went in to see how she was, and at eleven-thirty I said goodnight. I went home and slept for ten hours. Had it not been for Nancy and Charley Ellis I would have gone on a ten-day drunk. But during those ten days I met a fine girl, and in December of that year we were married and we stayed married for sixteen years, until she died. As the Irish would say, she died on me, and it was the only unkind thing she ever did to anyone.

The way things tie up, one with another, is likely to go unnoticed unless a lawyer or a writer calls our attention to it. And sometimes both the writer and the lawyer have some difficulty in holding things together. But if they are men of purpose they can manage, and fortunately for writers they are not governed by rules of evidence or the whims of the court. The whim of the reader is all that need concern a writer, and even that should not concern him unduly; Byron, Scott, Milton and Shakespeare, who have been quoted in this chronicle, are past caring what use I make of their words, and at the appointed time I shall join them and the other millions of writers who have said their little say and then become forever silent—and in the public domain. I shall join them with all due respect, but at the first sign of a patronizing manner I shall say: "My dear sir, when you were drinking it up at the Mermaid Tavern, did you ever have the potman bring a telephone to your table?"

I belonged to the era of the telephone at the tavern table, and the thirty-foot extension cord that enabled the tycoon to talk and walk, and to buy and sell and connive and seduce at long distances. It is an era already gone, and I may live to see the new one, in which extra-sensory perception combines with transistors, enabling the tycoon to dispense with the old-fashioned cord and *think* his way into new power and new beds. I may see the new era, but I won't belong to it. The writer of those days to come will be able to tune in on the voice of Lincoln at Gettysburg and hear the clanking of pewter mugs at the Mermaid, but he will never know the feeling of accomplishment that comes with the successful changing of a typewriter ribbon. A writer belongs to his time, and mine is past. In the days or years that remain to me, I shall entertain myself in contemplation of my time and be fascinated by the way things tie up, one with another.

I was in Boston for the tryout of a play I had written, and Charley Ellis's father had sent me a guest card to his club. "The old man said to tell you to keep your ears open and be sure and bring back any risqué stories you hear."

"At the Somerset Club?"

"The best. Where those old boys get them, I don't know, but that's where they tell them."

I used the introduction only once, when I went for a walk to get away from my play and everyone con-

cerned with it. I stood at the window and looked out at
the Beacon Street traffic, read a newspaper, and wandered to a small room to write a note to Mr. Ellis. There
was only one other man in the room, and he looked up
and half nodded as I came in, then resumed his letter-
writing. A few minutes later there was a small angry
spatter and I saw that a book of matches had exploded
in the man's hand. "*Son* of a *bitch!*" he said.

His left hand was burned and he stared at it with
loathing.

"Put some butter on it," I said.

"What?"

"I said, put some butter on it."

"I've heard of tea, but never butter."

"You can put butter on right away, but you have to
wait for the water to boil before you have tea."

"What's it supposed to do?"

"Never mind that now. Just put it on. I've used it.
It works."

He got up and disappeared. He came back in about
ten minutes. "You know, it feels much better. I'd never
heard of butter, but the man in the kitchen had."

"It's probably an old Irish remedy," I said.

"Are you Irish?"

"Yes. With the name Malloy I couldn't be anything else."

"Howdia do. My name is Hackley. Thanks very much. I wonder what it does, butter?"

"It does something for the skin. I guess it's the same principle as any of the greasy things."

"Of course. And it's cooling. It's such a stupid accident. I thought I closed the cover, but I guess I didn't." He hesitated. "Are you stopping here?"

"No, staying at the Ritz, but I have a guest card from Mr. Ellis in New York."

"Oh, of course. Where did you know *him?*"

"His son is a friend of mine."

"You're a friend of Charley's? I see. He's had another child, I believe. A daughter, this time."

"Yes. They wanted a daughter. I'm one of the godfathers of the boy."

"Oh, then you know him very well."

"Very," I said.

"I see. At Harvard?"

"No, after college. Around New York."

"Oh, yes. Yes," he said. Then: "Oh, *I* know who you

are. You're the playwright. Why, I saw your play night
before last."

"That wasn't a very good night to see it," I said.

"Oh, I didn't think it was so bad. Was I right in thinking that one fellow had trouble remembering his lines?
The bartender?"

"Indeed you were."

"But aside from that, I enjoyed the play. Had a few
good chuckles. That what-was-she, a chorus girl? They
do talk that way, don't they? It's just that, uh, when you
hear them saying those things in front of an audience.
Especially a Boston audience. You know how we are.
Or do you? We look about to see how the others are taking it. Tell me, Mr. Malloy, which do you prefer? Writing books, or writing for the stage?"

"At the moment, books."

"Well, of course with an actor who doesn't remember
lines. A friend of mine in New York knows you. She sent
me two of your books. I think one was your first and
the other was your second."

"Oh? Who was that?"

"Polly Williamson is her name."

So here he was, the serious-minded widower who had

been Polly Williamson's only lover. "That was damn nice of Polly. She's a swell girl."

"You *like* Polly. So do I. Never see her, but she's a darn nice girl and I hear from her now and again. Very musical, and I like music. Occasionally she'll send me a book she thinks I ought to read. I don't always like what she likes, and she knows I won't, but she does it to stimulate me, you know."

I had an almost ungovernable temptation to say something coarse. Worse than coarse. Intimate and anatomical and in the realm of stimulation, about Polly in bed. Naturally he misread my hesitation. "However," he said. "I enjoyed your first book very much. The second, not quite as much. So you're James J. Malloy?"

"No, I'm not James J. Malloy. I'm James Malloy, but my middle initial isn't J."

"I beg your pardon. I've always thought it was James J."

"People do. Every Irishman has to be James J. or John J."

"No. There was John L. Sullivan," said Hackley.

"Oh, but he came from Boston."

"Indeed he did. But then there was James J. Wadsworth. I know he wasn't Irish."

"No, but he was sort of a friend of Al Smith's."

"*Was he really?* I didn't know that. Was—he—really? Could you by any chance be thinking of his father, James W. Wadsworth?"

"I am. Of course I am. The senator, James W. Wadsworth."

"Perfectly natural mistake," said Hackley. "Well, I have to be on my way, but it's been nice to've had this chat with you. And thank you for the first-aid. I'll remember butter next time I set myself on fire."

On the evening of the next day I was standing in the lobby of the theatre, chatting with the press agent of the show and vainly hoping to overhear some comment that would tell me in ten magic words how to make the play a success. It was the second intermission. A hand lightly touched my elbow and I turned and saw Polly Williamson. "Do you remember me?" she said.

"Of course I remember you. I told you once I'd never forget you." Then I saw, standing with but behind her, Mr. Hackley, and I was sorry I was quite so demonstrative. "Hello, Mr. Hackley. How's the hand?"

He held it up. "Still have it, thanks to you."

"Just so you can applaud long and loud."

"The bartender fellow is better tonight, don't you think?"

"Much better," I said. "I'm glad you can sit through it a second time."

"He has no choice," said Polly Williamson.

"I hadn't, either," said Hackley. "I'll have you know this lady came all the way from New York just to see your play."

"You did, Polly?"

"Well, yes. But I don't know that I ought to tell you why."

"Why did you?" I said.

"Well, I read excerpts from some of the reviews, and I was afraid it wouldn't reach New York."

"We've tightened it up a little since opening night. I think the plan is now to take it to Philadelphia. But it was awfully nice of you to come."

"I wouldn't have missed it. I'm one of your greatest fans, and I like to tell people I knew you when."

"Well, I like to tell people I know you."

"I suppose you're terribly busy after the show," said Hackley.

"Not so busy that I couldn't have a drink with Polly and you, if that's what you had in mind."

They waited for me in the Ritz Bar. Two tweedy women were sitting with them, but they got up and left before I reached the table. "I didn't mean to drive your friends away," I said.

"They're afraid of you. Frightened to death," said Hackley.

"They're pretty frightening themselves," I said, angrily.

"They are, but before you say any more I must warn you, one of them is *my* cousin *and* Charley Ellis's cousin," said Polly Williamson.

"They thought your play was frightful," said Hackley.

"Which should assure its success," said Polly. "Maisie, my cousin, goes to every play that comes to Boston and she hasn't liked anything since I don't know when."

"*The Jest,* with Lionel and Jack Barrymore, I think was the last thing she really liked. And not so much the play as Jack Barrymore."

"I don't think she'd *really* like John Barrymore," I said.

"Oh, but you're wrong. She met him, and she does," said Hackley. It seemed to me during the hour or more that we sat there that he exerted a power over Polly that was effortless on his part and unresisted by her. He never allowed himself to stay out of the conversation, and Polly never finished a conversational paragraph that he chose to interrupt. I was now sure that their affair was still active, in Boston. She had occasion to remark that he never went to New York, which led me to believe that the affair was conducted entirely on his home ground, on his terms, and at as well as for his pleasure. I learned that he lived somewhere in the neighborhood—two or three minutes' walk from the hotel; and that she always stayed with an aunt who lived on the other side of the Public Garden. Since they had not the slightest reason to suspect that I knew any more about them than they had told me, they unconsciously showed the whole pattern of their affair. It was a complete reversal of the usual procedure, in which the Boston man goes to New York to be naughty. Polly went to Boston under the most respectable auspices and with the most innocent excuses—and as though she were returning home to sin. (I did not pass that judgment on her.) Williamson was an ebullient, arrogant boor; Hackley was a Bostonian, who shared her love of music, painting, and flowers; and whatever they did in bed, it was almost certainly totally different from whatever she did with Williamson, which was not hard to guess at. I do know that in the dimly lighted bar of the hotel she seemed more genuinely at home and at ease than in her own house or at the New York parties where I would see her, with the odd difference that in Boston she was willingly under the domination of a somewhat epicene aesthete, while in New York she quietly but, over the years, noticeably resisted Williamson's habit of taking control of people's lives. After fifteen years of marriage to Williamson she was regarded in New York as a separate and individual woman, who owed less and less to her position as the wife of a spectacular millionaire. But none of that was discernible to me in her relations with Hackley. She did what he wanted to do, and in so doing she completed the picture of her that Charley Ellis had given me. In that picture, her man was missing. But now I saw that Hackley, not the absent Williamson, was her man.

It was hardly a new idea, that the lover was more husband than the husband; but I had never seen a case in which geography, or a city's way of life, had been so influential. Polly not only returned to Hackley; she returned to Boston and the way of life that suited her best and that Hackley represented. There was even something appropriately austere about her going back to New York and Williamson. Since divorce was undesirable, with Williamson, the multi-millionaire, she was making-do. The whole thing delighted me. It is always a pleasure to discover that someone you like and have underestimated on the side of simplicity turns out to be intricate and therefore worthy of your original interest. (Intricacy in someone you never liked is, of course, just another reason for disliking him.)

"I have to go upstairs now and start working on the third act," I said.

"Oh, I hope we didn't keep you," said Hackley.

"You did, and I'm very glad you did. The director and the manager have had an hour to disagree with each other. Now I'll go in and no matter what I say, one of them will be on my side and the other will be left out in the cold. That's why I prefer writing books, Mr. Hackley . . . Polly, it's been very nice to've seen you again. Spread the good word when you go back. Tell everybody it's a great play."

"Not great, but it's good," said Polly. "When will you be back in New York?"

"Leaving tomorrow afternoon."

"So am I. Maybe I'll see you on the train."

There was a situation in my play that plainly needed something to justify a long continuing affair, something other than an arbitrary statement of love. In the elevator it came to me: it was Polly's compromise. In continuing her affair with Hackley, Polly—and the woman in my play—would be able to make a bad marriage appear to be a good one. The character in the play was a movie actress, and if Polly saw the play again she never would recognize herself. The director, the manager, and I agreed that we would leave the play as-is in Boston, and open with the new material in Philadelphia. Only three members of the cast were affected by the new material, and they were quick studies. One of them was Julianna Moore.

I had said to my wife: "Would you object if I had Julie read for the part?"

"No. You know what I'd object to," she said.

"Well, it won't happen. There won't be any flare-up.

Kenworthy is doing the sets, and they seem to be making a go of it."

There was no flare-up. Julie worked hard and well and got good notices in Boston, and I got used to having her around. I suppose that if she had come to my room in the middle of the night, my good intentions would have vanished. But we had discussed that. "If people that have slept together can never again work together," she said, "then the theatre might as well fold up. They'd never be able to cast a play on Broadway. And as to Hollywood . . ."

"Well, if you get too attractive, I'll send for my wife," I said.

"You won't have to. Ken will be there most of the time," she said. "Anyway, Jim, give me credit for some intelligence. I know you thought this all out and talked it over with your wife. Well, *I* talked it over with Ken, too. He hates you, but he respects you."

"Then we're in business," I said, and that was really all there was to it. I made most of my comments to the actors through the director, and Julie was not the kind of woman or actress who would use acquaintance with the author to gain that little edge.

Polly Williamson was at the Back Bay station and we got a table for two in the diner. "Do you think Mr. Willkie has a chance?" she said.

"I think he did have, but not now. Roosevelt was so sure he was a shoo-in that he wasn't going to campaign, and that was when Willkie had his chance. But luckily I was able to persuade the President to make some speeches."

"You did?"

"Not really," I said. "But I did have a talk with Tim Cochran in August, and I told him that Roosevelt was losing the election. I was very emphatic. And then one of the polls came out and showed I was right."

"Are you a New Dealer? I suppose you are."

"All the way."

"Did you ever know Jack Preswell? I know you know Nancy, Nancy Ellis, but did you know her first husband?"

"I once went to a baseball game with him, that's all."

"That's a tragic story. You know how he was killed and all that, I'm sure, but the real tragedy happened several years before. Jack was a brilliant student in Law School and something of an idealist. He had a job with

Carson, Cass & Devereux, but he quit it to get into the
New Deal. I probably shouldn't be saying this . . ."

"You can say anything to me."

"Well, I *want* to. Nancy is married to my cousin and I
know you and he are very good friends, but all is far
from well there, you know."

"No, I didn't know. I haven't seen them lately."

"Nancy and her father hounded Jack Preswell. They
were very contemptuous of his ideals, and when he
went to Washington Nancy wouldn't go with him. She
said it would be a repudiation of everything she believed in and her father believed in and everything
Jack's *family* believed in. As a woman I think Nancy was
just looking for an excuse. Nancy is *so* beautiful and
has been told so *so* many times that she'd much rather
be admired for her brains. Consequently she can be very
intolerant of other people's ideas, and she made Jack's
life a hell. Not that Jack was any rose. I didn't agree
with him, but he had a perfect right to count on Nancy's
support, and he never got it. Not even when he got out
of the New Deal. She should have stuck by him, at
least publicly."

"Yes, as it turned out, Preswell became as anti-New

Deal as she was, or Old Man McMinnies. I knew a little about this, Polly."

"Well, did I tell it fairly? I don't think you could have known much of it, because she was at her worst in front of his friends. She's a very destructive girl, and now she's up to the same old tricks with Charley. You don't know *that*, do you?"

"No."

"She's gotten Charley into America First. You knew that?"

"No, I didn't."

"Yes. And even my husband, as conservative as he is, and his father, they've stayed out of it. What's the use of isolationism now, when we're practically in it already? I agree with you, I think Roosevelt's going to win, although I just can't vote for him. But he'll get in and then it's only a question of another *Lusitania*, and we'll be in it too. So I don't see the practical value of America First. We ought to be getting stronger and stronger and the main reason I won't vote for Mr. Roosevelt is that he's such a hypocrite. He won't come out and honestly say that we're headed toward war."

"A little thing about neutrality and the head of the United States government."

"Oh, come. Do you think Hitler and Mussolini are hoping for a last-minute change of heart? Roosevelt should be uniting the country instead of playing politics. This nonsense about helping the democracies is sheer hypocrisy. There is no France, there's only England."

"You're very fiery, Polly."

"Yes. We have two English children staying with us. Their father was drowned coming back from Dunkerque. Nancy has Charley convinced that their presence in our house is a violation of neutrality. She said it wouldn't be fashionable to have two German children. When have I ever given a darn about fashion? That really burned me up."

I became crafty. "How do they feel about this in Boston? What does Mr. Hackley think?"

"Ham? The disappointment of his life was being turned down by the American Field Service. He'd have been wonderful, too. Speaks French, German, and Italian, and has motored through all of Europe. He'd make a wonderful spy."

"They'd soon catch on to him."

"Why?"

"If he burnt his hand, he'd say 'Son of a bitch,' and they'd know right away he was an American."

"Oh, yes." She smiled. "He told me about that. He's nice, don't you think?"

She was so nearly convincingly matter-of-fact. "Yes. He and I'd never be friends, but of his type I like him. Solid Boston."

"I don't know," she said. "Charley's almost that, and you and he have been friends quite a long time. Poor Charley. I don't know what I hope. Oh, I do. I want him to be happy with Nancy. I just hate to see what I used to like in him being poisoned and ruined by that girl."

"And you think it is?"

"The Charley Ellis I used to know would have two English children staying with him, and he'd probably be in the Field Service, if not actually in the British army."

"Well, my wife and I haven't taken any English children, and I'm not in the Field Service, so I can't speak. However, I'm in agreement with you in theory about the war. And in sentiment."

"Look up Charley after your play opens. Talk to him."

"Do you think I'd get anywhere in opposition to Nancy?"

"Well, you can have a try at it," she said.

I did have a try at it, after my play opened to restrained enthusiasm and several severe critical notices. Charley and I had lunch one Saturday and very nearly his opening remark was: "I hear you caught up with Polly and her bosom companion?"

I was shocked by the unmistakable intent of the phrase. "Yes, in Boston," I said.

"Where else? He never leaves there. She nips up there every few weeks and comes home full of sweetness and light, fooling absolutely no one. Except herself. Thank God I didn't go to Oxford."

"Why?"

"Well, you saw Hackley. He went to Oxford—after Harvard, of course."

"You sound as if you had a beef against Harvard, too."

"There are plenty of things I don't like about it, beginning with der Fuehrer, the one in the White House," he said. "Polly fill you up with sweetness and light, and tell you how distressed she was over Nancy and me?"

"No, we had my play to talk about," I said.

"Well, she's been sounding off. She's imported a couple of English kids and gives money to all the British causes. She'd have done better to have a kid by Hackley, but maybe they don't *do* that."

"What the hell's the matter with you, Charley? If I or anyone else had said these things about Polly a few years ago, you'd have been at their throat."

"That was before she began saying things about Nancy, things that were absolutely untrue, and for no reason except that Nancy has never gone in for all that phony Thoreau stuff. Nature-lover stuff. You know, I think Polly has had us all fooled from 'way back. You fell for it, and so did I, but I wouldn't be surprised if she'd been screwing Hackley all her life. One of those children that Junior thinks is his, *could* very well be Hackley's. The boy."

"Well, I wouldn't know anything about that. I've never seen their children. But what turned you against Polly? Not the possibility of her having had a child by Hackley."

"I've already told you. She's one of those outdoor-girl types that simply can't tolerate a pretty woman. And she's subtle, I'll give her that. She puts on this act of long-suffering faithful wife, while Junior goes on the make, and of course meanwhile Polly is getting hers in Boston."

"But you say not getting away with it."

"She got away with it for a long time, but people aren't that stupid. Even Junior Williamson isn't that stupid. He told Nancy that he's known about it for years, but as long as she didn't interfere with his life, he might as well stay married to her. Considering the nice stories Polly spread about Preswell and Nancy, I think Nancy showed considerable restraint in not making any cracks about Hackley and Polly's son. Nancy has her faults, but she wouldn't hurt an innocent kid."

The revised portraits of Junior Williamson, tolerating his wife's infidelity for years, and of Nancy Ellis, withholding gossip to protect a blameless child, were hard to get accustomed to. I did not try very hard. I was so astonished to see what a chump Nancy had made of my old friend, and so aggrieved by its effect on him, that I cut short our meeting and went home. Three or four months later the war news was briefly interrupted to make room for the announcement that Mrs. Ethridge Williamson, Jr., had established residence in Reno, Nevada. "A good day's work, Nancy," I said aloud. Much less surprising, a few months later, was the news item that Mrs. Smithfield Williamson, former wife of Ethridge Williamson, Jr., millionaire sportsman and financier, had married Hamilton Hackley, prominent Boston art and music patron, in Beverly, Massachusetts. The inevitable third marriage did not take place until the summer of 1942, when Lieutenant Commander Williamson, USNR, married Ensign Cecilia G. Reifsnyder, of the Women Accepted for Volunteer Emergency Service, in Washington, D. C. It seemed appropriate that the best man was Lieutenant Charles Ellis, USNR. The bride's only attendant was her sister, Miss Belinda Reifsnyder, of Catasauqua, Pennsylvania. I gave that six months, and it lasted twice that long.

My war record adds up to a big, fat nothing, but for a time I was a member of an Inverness-and-poniard organization, our elaborate nickname for cloak-and-dagger. In Washington I moved about from "Q" Building to the Brewery to South Agriculture and houses that were only street addresses. One day in 1943 I was on my way out of "Q" after an infuriatingly frustrating meeting with an advertising-man-turned-spy, a name-dropper who often got his names a little bit wrong. In the corridor a man fell in step with me and addressed me by my code nickname, which was Doc. "Do I know you?" I said.

"The name is Ham," said Hackley.

"We can't be too careful," I said.

"Well, we can't, as a matter of fact, but you can relax. I called you Doc, didn't I?" He smiled and I noticed that he needed dental work on the lower incisors. He had grown a rather thick moustache, and he had let his hair go untrimmed. "Come have dinner with Polly and me."

"I can think of nothing I'd rather do," I said.

"Irritating bastard, isn't he?" he said, tossing his head backward to indicate the office I had just left.

"The worst. The cheap, pompous worst," I said.

"One wonders, one wonders," said Hackley.

We got a taxi and went to a house in Georgetown. "Not ours," said Hackley. "A short-term loan from some friends."

Polly was a trifle thick through the middle and she had the beginnings of a double chin, but her eyes were clear and smiling and she was fitting into the description of happy matron.

"You're not at all surprised to see me," I said.

"No. I knew you were in the organization. Charley told me you'd turn up one of these days."

"Charley Who?"

"Heavens, have you forgotten all your old friends? Charley Ellis. Your friend and my cousin."

"I thought he was at CINCPAC."

"He's back and forth," she said. She put her hand on her husband's arm. "I wish this man got back as often. Would you like to see Charley? He's not far from here."

"Yes, but not just now. Later. I gather you're living in Boston?"

"Yes. My son is at Noble's and my daughter is still home with me. How is your lovely wife? I hear nothing but the most wonderful things about her. Aren't we lucky? Really, aren't we?"

"We are that," I said. Hackley had not said a word. He smoked incessantly, his hand was continually raising or lowering his cigarette in a slow movement that reminded me of the royal wave. I remembered the first time I had seen him and Polly together, when he would tack on his own thought to everything she said. "Are you still with us?" I said.

"Oh, very much so," he said.

"Can you tell Jim what you've been doing?"

"Well, now that's very indiscreet, Polly. Naturally he infers that I've told you, and he could report me for that. And should," said Hackley. "However, I think he can be trusted. He and I dislike the same man, and that's a great bond."

"And we like the same woman," I said.

"Thank you," said Polly.

"I've been in occupied territory," said Hackley. "Hence the hirsute adornment, the neglected teeth. I can't get my teeth fixed because I'm going back, and the Gestapo would take one look at the inside of my mouth and ask me where I'd happened to run across an American dentist. Hard question to answer. So I've been sitting here literally sucking on a hollow tooth. Yes, I'm still with you."

"I wish I were with *you*—not very much, but a little."

"You almost were, but you failed the first requirement. I had to have someone that speaks nearly perfect French, and you took Spanish."

"I'm highly complimented that you thought of me at all. I wish I did speak French."

"Yes, the other stuff you could have learned, as I had to. But without the French it was no go. French French. Not New Orleans or New Hampshire."

"Do you go in by parachute—excuse me, I shouldn't ask that."

"You wouldn't have got an answer," said Hackley. He rose. "I wonder if you two would excuse me for about an hour? I'd like to have a bath and five minutes' shut-eye."

As soon as he left us Polly ceased to be the happy matron. "He's exhausted. I wish they wouldn't send him back. He's over fifty, you know. I wish they'd take me, but do you know why they won't? The most complicated reasoning. The French would think I was a German agent, planted in France to spy on the Resistance. And the Germans would know I was English or American, because I don't speak German. But imagine the French thinking I was a German. My coloring, of course, and I *am* getting a bit dumpy."

"Where are your English children?"

"One died of leukemia, and their mother asked to have the other sent back, which was done. John Winant helped there. The child *is* better off with her mother, and the mother is too, I'm sure."

"Ham wants to go back, of course," I said.

"I wonder if he really does. Every time he goes back, his chances—and the Germans are desperate since we invaded Italy. It's young men's work, but a man of Ham's age attracts less attention. Young men are getting scarcer in France. Oh, I'm worried and I can't pretend I'm not. I can to Ham, but that's because I have to. But you saw how exhausted he is, and he's had—"

"Don't tell me. You were going to tell me how long he's been home. Don't. I don't want to have that kind of information."

"Oh, I understand. There's so little I want to talk about that I'm permitted to. Well, Charley Ellis is a safe subject. Shall I ask him to come over after dinner?"

"First, brief me on Charley and Nancy. I haven't seen him for at least a year."

"Nancy is living in New York, or you could be very sure I'd never see Charley. I didn't want to ever again. It was Nancy that stirred up the trouble between Junior

and me, and I'm very grateful to her now but I wasn't
then. Junior'd had lady friends, one after another, for
years and years, and if he'd been a different sort of man
it would have been humiliating. But as Charley pointed
out to me, oh, twenty years ago, there are only about
half a dozen Junior Williamsons in this country, and
they make their own rules. So, in order to survive, I
made mine, too. I really led a double life, the one as
Mrs. Ethridge Williamson, Junior, and the other, obviously, as Ham's mistress. You knew that, didn't you?"

"Well, yes."

"I didn't take anything away from Junior that he
wanted. Or withhold anything. And several times over
the years I did stop seeing Ham, when Junior would be
going through one of his periods of domesticity. I was
always taken in by that, and Junior can be an attractive man. To women. He has no men friends, do you
realize that? He always has some toady, or somebody
that he has to see a lot of because of business or one
of his pet projects. But he has no real men friends.
Women of all ages, shapes, and sizes and, I wouldn't
be surprised, colors. He married that Wave, and the
next thing I heard was she caught him in bed with her

sister. Why not? One meant as much to him as the other, and I'm told they were both pretty. That would be enough for Junior. A stroke of luck, actually. He's paying off the one he married. A million, I hear. And she's not going to say anything about her sister. What will those girls do with a million dollars? And think how much more they would have asked for if they'd ever been to the house on Long Island. But I understand he never took her there. That's what he considers home, you know. Christmas trees, and all the servants' children singing carols, and the parents lining up for their Christmas cheques. But the Wave was never invited. Oh, well, he's now an aide to an admiral, which should make life interesting."

"Having your commanding officer toady to you?"

"That, yes. But being able to pretend that you're just an ordinary commander, or maybe he's a captain now, but taking orders and so on. An admiral that would have him for an aide is the kind that's feathering his nest for the future, so I don't imagine Junior has any really unpleasant chores."

"Neither has the admiral. He's chair-borne at Pearl."

"Yes, Charley implied as much. I've talked too much

about Junior, and you want to know about Charley and Nancy. Well, Nancy stirred up the trouble. I never would have denied that I was seeing Ham, if Junior'd asked me, but that isn't what he asked me. He asked me if Ham were the father of our son, and I felt so sick at my stomach that I went right upstairs and packed a bag and took the next train to Boston, not saying a single word. When I got to my aunt's house, Junior was already there. He'd flown in his own plane. He said, 'I asked you a question, and I want an answer. *Entitled* to an answer.' So I said, 'The answer to the question is no, and I never want to say another word to you.' Nor have I. If he was entitled to ask the question, which I don't concede, he was entitled to my answer. He got it, and all communication between us since then has been through the lawyers."

"What about Nancy, though?"

"Oh, bold as brass, she told people that she thought my son's father was Ham. Which shows how well she doesn't know old Mr. Williamson. The boy looks exactly like his grandfather, even walks like him. But she also didn't know that Mr. Williamson is devoted to the boy, wouldn't speak to Junior for over a year, and worst of all, from Mr. Williamson's point of view, I have my son twelve months of the year and at school in Boston, so his grandfather has to come to Boston to see him. I refuse to take him to Long Island. And Mr. Williamson says I'm perfectly right, after Junior's nasty doubts. Doubts? Accusations."

"But you and Charley made it up," I said.

"Yes and no. Oh, we're friends again, but it'll never be what it used to be. Shall I tell you about it? You may be able to write it in a story sometime."

"Tell me about it."

"Charley was getting ready to ship out, his first trip to the Pacific, and he wrote me a letter. I won't show it to you. It's too long and too—private. But the gist of it was that if anything happened to him, he didn't want me to remember him unkindly. Then he proceeded to tell me some things that he'd said about me, that I hadn't heard, and believe me, Jim, if I'd ever heard them I'd have remembered him *very* unkindly. He put it all down, though, and then said, 'I do not believe there is a word of truth in any of these things.' Then he went on to say that our friendship had meant so much to him and so forth."

"It does, too, Polly," I said.

"Oh, James Malloy, you're dissembling. You know what he really said, don't you?"

"You're dissembling, too. I know what he used to feel."

"*I* never did. I always thought he was being extra kind to an awkward younger cousin," she said. "And he never liked Junior. Well, since you've guessed, or always knew, you strange Irishman, I'll tell you the rest. I wrote to him and told him our friendship was just where it had always been, and that I admired him for being so candid. That I was hurt by the things he had said, but that his first loyalty was to Nancy. That I never wanted to see Nancy again, and that therefore I probably would never see him. But since we lived such different lives, in different cities, I probably wouldn't see him anyway, in war or peace."

"But you did see him."

"Yes. We're friends again. I've seen him here in Washington. We have tea together now and then. To some extent it's a repetition of my trips to Boston to see Ham. Needless to say, with one great difference. I never have been attracted to Charley that way. But I'm his

double life, and the piquancy, such as it is, comes from
the fact that Nancy doesn't know we see each other.
Two middle-aged cousins, more and more like the
people that come to my aunt's house in Louisburg
Square."

"Do you remember the time we came down from
Boston?"

"Had dinner on the train. Of course."

"You said then, and I quote, that all was far from
well between Nancy and Charley."

She nodded. "It straightened itself out. It wasn't any
third party or anything of that kind. It was Nancy re-
shaping Charley to her own ways, and Charley putting
up a fight. But she has succeeded. She won. Except for
one thing that she could never understand."

"Which is?"

"That Charley and I like to have tea together. If she
found out, and tried to stop it, that's the one way she'd
lose Charley. So she mustn't find out. You see, Jim, I
don't want Charley, as a lover or as a husband. I have
my husband and he was my lover, too. As far as I'm
concerned, Charley is first, last and always a cousin.
A dear one, that I hope to be having tea with when

we're in our seventies. But that's all. And that's really what Charley wants, too, but God pity Nancy if she tries to deprive him of that."

For a little while neither of us spoke, and then she said something that showed her astuteness. "I'll give you his number, but let's not see him tonight. He doesn't like to be discussed, and if he came over tonight he'd know he had been."

"You're right," I said. "Polly, why did you divorce Williamson?"

"You're not satisfied with the reason I gave you?"

"It would be a good enough reason for some women, but not for you."

She looked at me and said nothing, but she was disturbed. She fingered her circle of pearls, picked up her drink and put it down without taking a sip.

"Never mind," I said. "I withdraw the question."

"No. No, don't. You gave me confidence one day when I needed it. The second time I ever saw you. I'll tell you."

"Not if it's an ordeal," I said.

"It's finding the words," she said. "The day Junior asked me point-blank if he was the father of my son,

I had just learned that I was pregnant again. By him, of course. One of his periods of domesticity. So I had an abortion, something I'd sworn I'd never do, and I've never been pregnant since. I had to have a hysterectomy, and Ham and I did want a child. You see, I couldn't answer your question without telling you the rest of it."

After the war my wife and I saw the Ellises punctiliously twice every winter; they would take us to dinner and the theatre, we would take them. Dinner was always in a restaurant, where conversation makes itself, and in the theatre it was not necessary. Charley and I, on our own, lunched together every Saturday at his club or mine, with intervals of four months during the warm weather and time out for vacations in Florida or the Caribbean. Every five years on Charley's birthday they had a dance in the ballroom of one of the hotels, and I usually had a party to mark the occasion of a new book or play. We had other friends, and so had the Ellises, and the two couples had these semi-annual evenings together only because not to do so would have been to call pointed attention to the fact that the only friendship was that of Charley and me. Our wives, for example, after an early exchange of lunches never had lunch together again; and if circumstances put me alone with Nancy, I had nothing to say. In the years of our acquaintance she had swung from America First to Adlai Stevenson, while I was swinging the other way. She used the word valid to describe everything but an Easter bonnet, another favorite word of hers was denigrate, and still another was challenge. When my wife died Nancy wrote me a note in which she "questioned the validity of it all" and told me to "face the challenge." When I married again she said I had made the only valid decision by "facing up to the challenge of a new life." I had ceased to be one of the authors she admired, and in my old place she had put Kafka, Kierkegaard, Rilke, and Camus. I sent her a copy of Kilmer to make her velar collection complete, but she did not think it was comical or cute.

Charley and I had arrived at a political rapprochement: he conceded that some of the New Deal had turned out well, I admitted that Roosevelt had been something less than a god. Consequently our conversations at lunch were literally what the doctor ordered

for men of our age. To match my Pennsylvania remi-
niscences he provided anecdotes about the rich, but to
him they were not the rich. They were his friends and
enemies, neighbors and relatives, and it was a good thing
to hear about them as such. Charley Ellis had observed
well and he remembered, and partly because he was
polite, partly because he had abandoned the thought
of writing as a career, he gave me the kind of information I liked to hear.

We seldom mentioned Nancy and even less fre-
quently, Polly. If he continued to have tea with her, he
did not say so. But one day in the late Forties we were
having lunch at his club and he bowed to a carefully
dressed man who limped on a cane and wore a patch
over his left eye. He was about sixty years old. "One
of your boys," said Charley.

"You mean Irish?"

"Oh, no. I meant O.S.S."

"He must have been good. The Médaille Militaire.
That's one they don't hand out for traveling on the
French Line."

"A friend of Ham Hackley's. He told me how Hackley
died."

All I knew was that Hackley had never come back from France after my evening with him in Washington. "How did he?" I said.

"The Germans caught him with a wad of plastic and a fuse wire in his pocket. He knew what he was in for, so he took one of those pills."

"An 'L' pill," I said.

"Whatever it is that takes about a half a minute. You didn't know that about Ham?"

"I honestly didn't."

"That guy, the one I just spoke to, was in the same operation. He blew up whatever they were supposed to blow up, but he stayed too close and lost his eye and smashed up his leg. You wouldn't think there was that much guts there, would you? He knew he couldn't get very far, but he set off the damn plastic and hit the dirt." Charley laughed. "Do you know what he told us? He said, 'I huddled up and put my hands over my crotch, so I lost an eye. But I saved everything else.' We got him talking at a club dinner this winter."

"I wish I'd been here."

"Not this club. This was at the annual dinner of my

club at Harvard. He was a classmate of Ham's. I don't usually go back, but I did this year."

"Did you see Polly?"

"Yes, I went and had tea with her. Very pleasant. Her boy gets out of Harvard this year. Daughter's married."

"We got an announcement. What does Polly do with her time?"

"Oh, why, I don't know. She always has plenty of things to do in Boston. A girl like Polly, with all her interests, she'd keep herself very busy. I must say she's putting on a little weight."

"What would she be now?"

"How old? Polly is forty-one, I think."

"Still young. Young enough to marry again."

"I doubt if she will," said Charley. "I doubt it very much. Boston isn't like New York, you know. In New York a woman hates to go to a party without a man, but in Boston a woman like Polly goes to a party by herself and goes home by herself and thinks nothing of it."

"Nevertheless she ought to have a husband. She's got a good thirty years ahead of her. She ought to marry if only for companionship."

"Companionship? Companionship is as hard to find as

love. More so. Love can sneak up on you, but when
you're looking for companionship you shop around."

"Maybe that's what Polly's doing, having a look at
the field."

"Maybe. There's one hell of a lot of money that goes
with her, and she's not going to marry a fortune-hunter.
Oh, I guess Polly can take care of herself."

"Just out of curiosity, how *much* money is there?"

"How much money? Well, when Polly's father died,
old Mr. Smithfield, he left five million to Harvard, and
another million to a couple of New York hospitals, and
a hundred thousand here and a hundred thousand there.
I happen to know that he believed in tithes. All his life
he gave a tenth of his income to charity. So if he fol-
lowed that principle in his will, he was worth around
seventy million gross. I don't know the taxes on that
much money, but after taxes it all went to Polly. In ad-
dition, Ham Hackley left her all his money, which was
nothing like Cousin Simon Smithfield's, but a tidy sum
nonetheless. I also know that when Polly divorced
Junior Williamson, old Mr. Williamson changed his
will to make sure that the grandchildren would each get
one-third, the same as Junior. That was quite a blow to

Junior. So all in all, Polly's in a very enviable position, financially."

"Good God," I said. "It embarrasses me."

"Why you?"

"Don't you remember that day I told her I loved her?"

"Oh, yes. Well, she took that as a compliment, not as a business proposition. She's never forgotten it, either."

"Well, I hope Polly holds on to her good sense. When I was a movie press agent I made a great discovery that would have been very valuable to a fortune-hunter. And in fact a few of them had discovered it for themselves. Big stars, beautiful and rich, would come to New York and half the time they had no one to take them out. They depended on guys in the publicity department. I never would have had to work for a living."

"How long could you have stood that?"

"Oh, a year, probably. Long enough to get tired of a Rolls and charge accounts at the bespoke tailors. Then I suppose I'd have read a book and wished I'd written it. I knew a fellow that married a movie star and did all that, and he wasn't just a gigolo. He'd taught English at Yale. He took this doll for God knows how much, then she gave him the bounce and now he's living in Mexico.

He's had a succession of fifteen-year-old wives. Once every two or three years he comes to New York for a week. He subsists entirely on steak and whiskey. One meal a day, a steak, and all the whiskey he can drink. He's had a stroke and he knows he's going to die. I could have been that. In fact, I don't like to think how close I came."

"I don't see you as Gauguin."

"Listen, Gauguin wasn't unhappy. He was doing what he wanted to do. I don't see myself as Gauguin either. What I don't like to think of is how close I came to being my friend that married the movie actress. That I could have been."

"No, you were never really close. You were no closer than I was to marrying Polly. You thought about it, just as I did about marrying Polly. But I wasn't meant to marry Polly, and you weren't meant to steal money from a movie actress and go on the beach in Mexico."

"Go on the beach? Why did you say that?"

"It slipped. I knew the fellow you're talking about. Henry Root?"

"Yes."

"Before he taught at Yale he had the great distinction of teaching me at Groton. You know why he *stopped* teaching at Yale? Bad cheques. Not just bouncing cheques. Forgeries. There was one for a thousand dollars signed Ethridge B. Williamson, Junior. That did it. He had Junior's signature to copy from, but that wasn't the way Junior signed his cheques. He always signed E. B. Williamson J R, so his cheques wouldn't be confused with his father's, which had Ethridge written out. Henry was a charming, facile bum, and a crook. You may have been a bum, but you were never a crook. Were you?"

"No, I guess I wasn't. I never cheated in an exam, and the only money I ever stole was from my mother's pocketbook. And got caught, every time. My mother always knew how much was in her purse."

"Now let me ask you something else. Do you think Henry Root would ever have been a friend of Polly's? As good a friend, say, as you are?"

"Well—I'd say no."

"And you'd be right. When she was Polly Smithfield he'd always give her a rush at the dances, and it was an understood thing that Junior and I would always cut in. I don't think we have to worry about Polly and fortune-hunters, or you about how close you came to being Henry Root. I don't even worry about how close that damn story of yours came to keeping Nancy from marrying me."

"Oh, that story. 'Christiana.' No. 'Telemark.' That was it, 'Telemark.' "

"You don't even remember your own titles, but that was the one."

"I may not remember the title, but the point of the story was that two people could take a chance on marriage without love."

"Yes, and Nancy was so convinced that you were wrong that she had it on her mind. You damn near ruined my life, Malloy."

"No I didn't."

"No, you didn't. My life was decided for me by Preswell, when he walked in front of that taxi."

I knew this man so well, and with his permission, but I had never heard him make such an outright declaration of love for his wife, and on my way home I realized that until then I had not known him at all. It was not a discovery to cause me dismay. What did he know about me? What, really, can any of us know about any of us, and why must we make such a thing of loneliness when it is the final condition of us all? And where would love be without it?

SALEM COLLEGE LIBRARY
ton-Salem, North Carolina